Ming and Her Poppy

Written by Deirdre Sullivan

Illustrated by Maja Löfdahl

Sky Pony Press
New York

To Dad, for always knowing the way. —D. S.

To all the grandfathers who helped, and to 三舅父 —M. L.

Sky Pony Press books may be purchased in bulk at special discount for sales promotion, corporate gifts, fund-raising, or educational purposes. Special editions can also be created to specifications.
For details, contact the Special Sales Department, Sky Pony Press, 307 West 36th Street, 11th Floor, New York, NY 10018 or info@skyhorsepublishing.com.

Sky Pony® is a registered trademark of Skyhorse Publishing, Inc.®, a Delaware corporation.

Visit our website at www.skyponypress.com
Books, authors, and more at www.skyponypressblog.com

10 9 8 7 6 5 4 3 2 1

Manufactured in China August 2017
This product conforms to CPSIA 2008.

Library of Congress Cataloging-in-Publication Data is available on file.

Cover design by Sammy Yuen
Cover illustration by Maja Löfdahl Green

Print ISBN: 978-1-5107-2943-8
eBook ISBN: 978-1-5107-2944-5

Thank you to everyone at Boston Photo Imaging and Sky Pony Press.

Ming and Poppy know their way

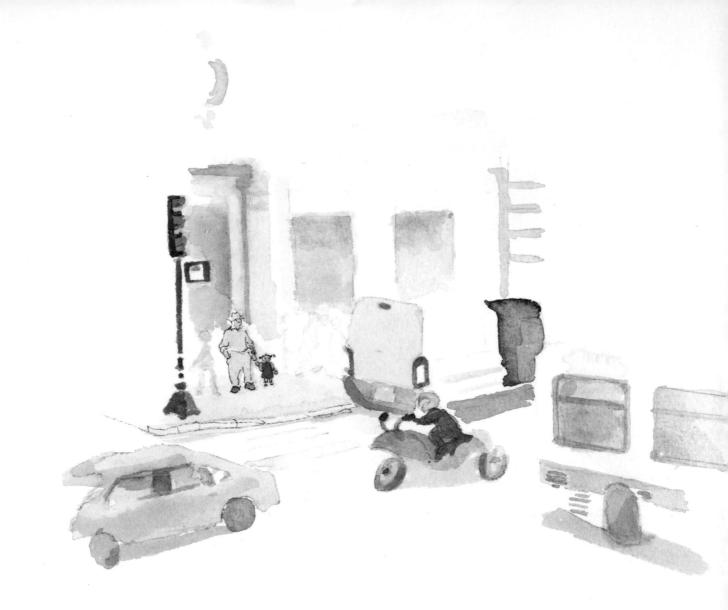

by tightly held hands

and story swapping,

by sidewalk cracks missed

and shadow dancing,

by sticks, by stones,
by names that sting,

and the purple night sky
tucking in the leaves.

Ming and Poppy know their way

by crowded crosswalks and honking horns,

by hello, how do you do's,
how are you's,
and flower boxes all in bloom,

by hop, by scotch, by wrought-iron fences,

by eyes closed tight
and wishes on pennies,

by criss-cross my heart
and pinky promises,

by cheerio, by toodle-oo,
by see you soon,

and two double scoops
of chocolate ice cream.